Brer Turkey Buzzard

Brer Wolf

Brer Terrapin

Brer Fox

Brer Marten

Brer Possum

BRER RABBIT HE SAYS THAT HE CAN GET THE BEST OF OLE BRER FOX ANY TIME O DAY.

This **BOOK**

belongs to

_____

BRER RABBIT
AND
BRER FOX

Retold by JANE SHAW
from the original of
JOEL CHANDLER HARRIS

Illustrated by
WILLIAM BACKHOUSE

Collins · Glasgow and London

CONTENTS

First published in this edition 1969
Seventh impression 1978
Published by William Collins Sons and Company Limited, Glasgow and London
© William Collins Sons and Company Limited
Printed in Great Britain

ISBN 0 00 138188 1

BRER FOX
*goes
a-hunting*

NCE there was an old Negro servant called Uncle Remus, who lived on a cotton plantation in America. It was Uncle Remus who told these tales of the Rabbit and the Fox and the other animals to a little boy.

"When Brer Fox hears how Brer Rabbit fools all the other animals in the neighbourhood," said Uncle Remus one evening, "he reckon, he did, that he better not be so bold, and he sort of let Brer Rabbit alone. By and by, they began to get kind of friendly with one another like they used to be, and it got so that Brer Fox would call on Brer Rabbit and they would sit up and smoke their pipes, they would, as if no harsh feelings had ever rested betwixt them.

At last one day Brer Fox comes along, all rigged out, and asks Brer Rabbit to go hunting with him, but Brer Rabbit, he feels lazy and he tells Brer Fox that he's got some other fish to fry. Brer Fox feel mighty sorry, but off he goes by himself. He was gone all day, and he had a monstrous stroke of luck, and he bagged a lot of game.

By and by, towards evening, Brer Rabbit sort of stretch himself, and allow it's almost time for Brer Fox to be getting along home. Then Brer Rabbit, he went and climbed up a tree-stump to see if he could hear Brer Fox coming. He ain't been there long, till, sure enough, here come

Brer Fox through the woods, singing and whistling. Brer Rabbit, he leap down off the stump, and lay in the road as if he was dead.

Brer Fox come along, and see Brer Rabbit lying there. He turn him over, he did, and examine him, and say, says he, 'This here rabbit's dead. He looks like he's been dead a long time. He's dead, but he's mighty fat. He's the fattest rabbit that I ever see, but he's been dead too long, I'm a-feared to take him home,' says he.

Brer Rabbit ain't saying nothing. Brer Fox, he licked his chops, but he went on and left Brer Rabbit lying in the road. Directly the Fox was out of sight, Brer Rabbit jump up, and run round through the woods and get in front of Brer Fox again. Brer Fox, he come up and there lay Brer Rabbit, apparently cold and stiff. Brer Fox, he look at Brer Rabbit, and he sort of think and study. After a while he slung his game-bag off his back and say to himself, says he, 'This here rabbit is just going to waste. I'll leave my game here, and I'll go back and get that other rabbit and with all the game I've caught, I'll make folks believe that I'm a mighty hunter,' says he.

And with that he dropped his game and loped back up the road after the other dead rabbit, and when he got out of sight old Brer Rabbit he snatch up Brer Fox's game and made off for home.

Next time he see Brer Fox he holler out, 'What did you catch the other day, Brer Fox?' says he.

Then Brer Fox holler back, 'I catch a handful of hard sense, Brer Rabbit,' says he.

Then old Brer Rabbit he laugh, he did, and up and respond, 'If I'd known you was after any of that, Brer Fox, I'd have lent you some of mine,' says he."

AGAINST THE LAW

"ONE day Brer Rabbit was going on one of his journeys," said Uncle Remus, "when first news you know he took and hear something holler, 'Oh, Lordy! Lordy! Won't somebody come help me?'

Brer Rabbit stop and listen. 'Twasn't long before something or other holler out: 'Lordy, lordy! Please, somebody come and help me!'

Brer Rabbit, he hoist up his ears, he did, and make answer back, 'Who is you, and what in the name of goodness is the matter?'

'Please, somebody, do run here!'

Brer Rabbit, he holler back, 'Whereabouts is you, and how come you there?'

'Do, please, somebody, run here and help a poor miserable creature! I'm down here in the big gully under this here great big rock!'

Brer Rabbit crept down to the big gully and look in, and who in the name of goodness d'you expect he see down there? Nobody in the round world but that there old Brer Wolf. He was lying down there in the big gully, and, bless gracious, 'pon top of him was a great big rock!

There he was, nearly mashed flat, but he got strength enough left to make folks hear him holler a mile off, and he holler so lonesome that it make Brer Rabbit feel mighty sorry, and no sooner does he feel sorry

than he hold his coat-tails out of the way and slid down the bank to see what he can do.

When he got down there, Brer Wolf ask him please, sir, can he help with the removance of that there rock, and Brer Rabbit allow he expect he can; and with that Brer Wolf holler and tell him for massy sake won't he whirl in and do it. Brer Rabbit took and catched hold of the rock and hump himself, and 'twasn't long before he get a purchase on it and, bless your soul, he lift it up.

It turn out that Brer Wolf ain't hurted much, and when he find this out, he took a notion that if he was ever going to get his revengeance out of Brer Rabbit, right then was the time, and no sooner does that come across his mind than he took and grab Brer Rabbit by the nape of the neck and the small of the back.

Brer Rabbit he kick and squeal, but it don't do no good, 'cause the more he kick, the tighter Brer Wolf clamp him, and squoze him so hard that Brer Rabbit was feared he was going to cut off his breath.

Brer Rabbit, he allow, 'Well, then, Brer Wolf! Is this the way you thank folks for saving your life?'

Brer Wolf grin big, and then he allow, 'I'll thank you, Brer Rabbit, and then I'll make fresh meat out of you.'

Brer Rabbit allow, 'If you talk that way, Brer Wolf, I never will do you another good turn whilst I live.'

Brer Wolf, he grin some more and say, 'That you won't, Brer Rabbit, that you won't! You won't do me a good turn till you're dead.'

Brer Rabbit sort of study to himself, he did, and then he allow, 'Where I come from, Brer Wolf, it's against the law for folks to kill them what done them a good turn, and I expect the law's the same right round these parts.'

Brer Wolf say he ain't so mighty sure about that. Brer Rabbit say he's willing to put the whole case before Brer Terrapin, and Brer Wolf say he's agreeable.

With that they make their way to where old Brer Terrapin stay, and when they get there, Brer Wolf he tell his side, and then Brer Rabbit he tell his side.

Old Brer Terrapin put on his specs and clear his throat, and then he allow, 'There's a mighty heap of mixedness in this here dispute, and before I can take any sides you'll just have to carry me to see the place whereabouts Brer Wolf was when Brer Rabbit found him,' says he.

Sure enough, they took and carried old Brer Terrapin down the big road till they come to the big gully and then they took him to where Brer Wolf got catched under the big rock. Old Brer Terrapin he walk round, he did, and poke at the place with the end of his cane. By and by he shook his head he did and allow, 'I hates to put you-all gents to so much trouble, yet there ain't two ways about it, I'll have to see just how Brer Wolf was catched, and just how the rock was lying on top of him,' says he.

Then Brer Wolf he lay down where he was when Brer Rabbit found

him, and then the others they up and roll the rock on top of him. They roll the rock on top of him and there he was. Brer Terrapin, he walk all round, and look at him. Then he sat down, he did, and make marks in the sand with his cane like he's thinking about something or other.

By and by Brer Wolf, he open up, 'Ow, Brer Terrapin! This here rock's getting mighty heavy!'

Brer Terrapin, he mark in the sand and study and study.

Brer Wolf holler, 'Ow, Brer Terrapin! This here rock is mashing the breath out of me!'

Brer Terrapin he says, says he, 'Brer Rabbit, you was in the wrong. You ain't had no business to come bothering Brer Wolf when he ain't bothering you. He was attending to his own business, and you ought to have been attending to yours.'

This make Brer Rabbit look ashamed of himself, but Brer Terrapin talk right along. 'When you was going down this here road this morning, you surely must have been a-going somewheres. If you *was* going somewheres, you better be going on. Brer Wolf, he wasn't going nowheres then and he ain't going nowheres now. You found him under that there rock and under that there rock you left him.'

And, bless gracious!" exclaimed Uncle Remus, "them there creatures racked off from there and left old Brer Wolf under that rock!"

MR. DOG'S
new
shoes

"WELL, then," said Uncle Remus, "there was one time when old Brer Rabbit was going to town after something or other for his family, and he was almost ashamed to go 'cause his shoes were teetotally worn out. Yet he wanted to go, so he put just as good a face on it as he can, and he take his walking-stick and set out just as big as the next one.

Well, then, old Brer Rabbit go on down the big road till he come to a place where some folks had been camping out the night before, and he sat down by the fire to warm his feet, 'cause the mornings were sort of cold, like these here mornings. He sat there and looked at his toes, and he feel mighty sorry for himself.

Well, then, he sat there, and it wasn't long before he hear something or other trotting down the road, and here come Mr. Dog a-smelling and a-snuffling round to see if the folks had left any scraps by the camp-fire. Mr. Dog was all dressed up in his Sunday-go-to-meeting clothes, and more than that, he had on brand new shoes.

When Brer Rabbit see them shoes he feel mighty bad, but he don't let on. He bow to Mr. Dog mighty polite, and Mr. Dog he bow back. Brer Rabbit, he say, 'Mr. Dog, where you going, all fixed up like this?'

'I'm going to town, Brer Rabbit. Where you going?'

'I thought I'd go to town myself to get me a new pair of shoes, 'cause my old ones are worn out and they hurt my foots so bad I can't wear them. Them mighty nice shoes that you got on, Mr. Dog; where you get 'em?'

'Down in town, Brer Rabbit, down in town.'

'They fits you mighty snug, Mr. Dog, and I wish you'd be so good as to let me try one of them on.'

Brer Rabbit talk so mighty sweet that Mr. Dog sat right flat on the ground and took off one of the behind shoes and lent it to Brer Rabbit. Brer Rabbit, he lope off down the road and then he come back. He tell Mr. Dog that the shoe fits mighty nice, but with one of them on, it make him trot lop-sided.

Well then, Mr. Dog, he pull off the other behind shoe and Brer Rabbit trot off and try it.

He come back, he did, and he say, 'They mighty nice, Mr. Dog, but they sort of raise me up behind and I dunno exactly how they feel.'

Mr. Dog want to be polite, and he took off the before shoes and Brer Rabbit put 'em on and stomp his foots and allow, 'Now that sort of feel like shoes.'

He rack off down the road and when he gets where he ought to turn round, he just lay back his ears and keep on going; and 'twasn't long before he get out of sight.

Mr. Dog he holler, and tell him to come back, but Brer Rabbit keep on going. Mr. Dog he holler, Mr. Rabbit he keep on going. And down to this day, Mr. Dog been a-running after Brer Rabbit, and if you'll just go out in the woods with any dog on this place, the minute he smells rabbit, he'll holler and tell him to come back."

BRER BUZZARD'S GOLD-MINE

"THERE was another man that was as smart as Brer Rabbit," said Uncle Remus one night.

"I thought the Rabbit was the smartest of them all," said the little boy dismally, for Brer Rabbit had become a sort of hero to him.

"It's like I tell you," said Uncle Remus. "There ain't no smart man, except that there's a smarter."

"Who fooled the Rabbit this time?" the little boy asked.

"In those days," said the old man, "the beastesses carried on matters same as folks. They went into farming, and they kept shop and had barbecues when the weather was agreeable. One time, Brer Rabbit and old Brer Turkey-Buzzard decided they'd go shares and harvest buckwheat together. It was a mighty good year, and the crop turn out monstrous well, but when the time came for dividing, it came to light that old Brer Buzzard ain't got nothing. The buckwheat was all gone, and there was nothing to show for it. Brer Rabbit, he made out that he was in a worse fix than Brer Buzzard, and he mope around as if he was ruined.

Brer Buzzard, he ain't saying nothing, but he keep up a monstrous

thinking, and one day he came along and tell Brer Rabbit that he done find a rich gold-mine just across the river.

'You come along with me, Brer Rabbit,' says Brer Turkey-Buzzard, 'and between the two of us we'll make short work of that gold-mine,' says he.

Brer Rabbit, he was mighty keen for the job, but he study and study, he did, how he's going to get across the water, because every time he gets his foot wet all the family catch cold. Then he asked Brer Buzzard what he could do, and Brer Buzzard he say that he'll carry Brer Rabbit across, and with that old Brer Buzzard he squat down, he did, and spread his wings, and Brer Rabbit mounted on his back and up they rose."

"What did the Buzzard do then?" asked the little boy.

"They rose," went on Uncle Remus, "and when they alighted, they alighted on the top of the highest pine-tree, and the pine-tree was growing on an island, and the island was in the middle of the river with deep water running all round. They had no sooner landed than Brer Rabbit, he know which way the wind is blowing and what old Brer Buzzard is planning, and by the time old Brer Buzzard got himself balanced on a branch, Brer Rabbit he up and say, says he, 'Whiles we are resting here,

Brer Buzzard, and seeing you've been so good, I got something to tell you,' says he. 'I got a gold-mine of my own, one that I made myself, and I 'spect we better go back to mine before we bother with yours,' says he.

Then old Brer Buzzard he laughed till he shake and Brer Rabbit sing out, 'Hold on, Brer Buzzard! Don't flap your wings when you laugh, because if you do, something will drop from up here, and my gold-mine won't do you any good, and neither will yours do me any good.'

But before they got down from there, Brer Rabbit told him all about the buckwheat, and he had to promise to divide fair and square. So Brer Buzzard, he carried him back, and Brer Rabbit he walk weak in the knees for a month afterwards.''

Brer Terrapin shows his STRENGTH

"**B**RER Terrapin was the wiliest man," said Uncle Remus, "he was the wiliest man of the whole gang. He was that.

One night there was a party in the neighbourhood to make candy, and so many neighbours came in response to the invite that they had to put the molasses in the wash-tub and build the fire in the yard. Brer Bear, he helped to bring in the wood, Brer Fox he mended the fire, Brer Wolf he kept the dogs off, Brer Rabbit he greased the bottom of the plates to keep the candy from sticking, and Brer Terrapin, he climbed up in a chair and said he'd see that the molasses didn't boil over.

Well then, whiles they were all a-sitting there and the molasses was a-boiling and a-bubbling, they began talking mighty biggity. Brer Rabbit, he say he's the swiftest; but Brer Terrapin he rock along in the chair and watch the molasses. Brer Fox he say he's the sharpest, but Brer Terrapin he rock along. Brer Bear he say he's the strongest, but Brer Terrapin he rock and he keep on rocking.

By and by he sort of shut one eye and say, says he, 'It look like the old hardshell ain't nowhere alongside this crowd, yet here I is, and I'm the same man that can show Brer Bear that he ain't the strongest,' says he.

Then they all laugh and holler, 'cause it look like Brer Bear is stronger

than an ox. By and by they up and ask how he was going to do it.

'Give me a good strong rope,' says Brer Terrapin, says he, 'and let me get in a puddle of water and then let Brer Bear see if he can pull me out,' says he.

They all laugh again and Brer Bear, he says, 'We ain't got no rope,' says he.

'No,' says Brer Terrapin, 'and neither have you got the strength,' and then Brer Terrapin he rock and rock along and watch the molasses a-boiling and a-bubbling.

After a while one of the neighbours up and say that she'd lend them a rope and while the candy was a-cooling on the plates, they could all go to the stream and see Brer Terrapin carry out his project. Brer Terrapin,'' continued Uncle Remus, ''wasn't much bigger than the palm of my hand, and it look mighty funny to hear him bragging about how he can outpull Brer Bear. But they get the rope after a while and then they all set off for the stream.

When Brer Terrapin find the place he wanted, he took one end of the

rope and gave the other to Brer Bear. 'Now then, ladies and gents,' says Brer Terrapin, 'you all go with Brer Bear up there in the woods and I'll stay here, and when you hear me holler, that's the time for Brer Bear to see if he can haul in the slack of the rope. You all take care of that there end,' says he, 'and I'll take care of this here end,' says he.

Then they all go off and left Brer Terrapin and when they were good and gone, he dived down into the water, he did, and tied the rope hard and fast to one of these here big roots, and then he rose up and gave a whoop.

Brer Bear he wrap the rope round his hand and wink, and with that he gave a big jerk, but Brer Terrapin didn't budge. Then he take both hands and give a big pull, but all the same Brer Terrapin didn't budge. Then he turn round, he did, and put the rope across his shoulders and try to walk off with Brer Terrapin, but Brer Terrapin look like he don't feel like walking. Then Brer Wolf he put in and help Brer Bear pull, but that made no difference, and then they all help him and bless gracious, whiles they was all a-pulling, Brer Terrapin he holler and ask them why they don't take up the slack. Then when Brer Terrapin feels them quit pulling, he dived down and untied the rope and by the time they got to the stream, Brer Terrapin he was sitting in the edge of the water just as natural as the next one.

Then he up and says, 'That last pull was a mighty stiff one and a little more and you'd have had me,' says he. 'You're monstrous strong, Brer Bear, and you pull like a yoke of oxen, but I sort of had the advantage of you,' says he.

Then Brer Bear, seeing as how his mouth begins to water for the sweetness, he up and say he expects that the candy is ready, and off they all go after it.''

Brer Rabbit
gets a
HOUSE

"YOU sit over there, and I'll sit over here," Uncle Remus said one evening to the little boy, "and I'll sort of rustle round with my remembrance and see if I can call to mind the tale about how old Brer Rabbit got himself a two-storey house without laying out much cash.

It turn out one time that a whole lot of the creatures took a notion that they'd go shares in building a house. Old Brer Bear, he was amongst them, and Brer Fox, and Brer Wolf, and Brer Coon and Brer Possum, right down to old Brer Mink. There was a whole parcel of them, and they whirl in and they build the house in less than no time. Brer Rabbit, he pretend it made his head swim to climb up on the scaffold, and likewise he say it makes him catch the palsy to work in the sun, but he stuck a pencil behind his ear and he went round measuring and marking; and he was that busy that the other creatures say to themselves that he's doing a monstrous sight of work; and folks going along the big road say Brer Rabbit's doing more hard work than the whole boiling lot of them. Yet all the time Brer Rabbit ain't doing nothing, he's just lying in the shade scratching fleas off himself. The other creatures, they build the house, and gentlemens! it was a fine one too. It had an upstairs and a downstairs and

chimneys all round, and it had rooms for all the creatures who went shares and help make it.

Brer Rabbit, he pick out one of the upstairs rooms and he took and got himself a gun, and one of these here brass cannons, and he put them in there when the other creatures ain't looking; and then he got himself a tub of nasty, dirty water, which likewise he put in there when they ain't looking. So then, when they get the house all fixed, and while they was all a-sitting in the parlour after supper, Brer Rabbit, he sort of yawn and stretch himself and say he believe he'll go to his room. When he got there, and while all the other creatures was a-laughing and a-chatting, Brer Rabbit he stick his head out of his room and sing out, 'When a big man like me wants to sit down, whereabouts he going to sit?' says he.

Then the creatures they laugh and holler back, 'If a big man like you can't sit in a chair, he better sit down on the floor.'

'Watch out down there, then,' says old Brer Rabbit, 'cause I'm a-going to sit down,' says he.

With that, *bang*! went Brer Rabbit's gun. 'Course, this sort of astonish the creatures, and they look round at one another as much as to say, 'What in the name of gracious is that?' They listen and listen, but they don't hear no more fuss, and it wasn't long before they got to chatting and jabbering some more.

By and by, Brer Rabbit stick his head out of the door and sing out, 'When a big man like me wants to cough, whereabouts he going to cough?'

Then the other creatures, they holler back, 'If a big man like you ain't a gone gump, he can cough anywhere he pleases.'

'Watch out down there then,' says Brer Rabbit, ''cause I'm going to turn loose a cough right here,' says he.

With that Brer Rabbit let off his cannon—*bulder-um-m-m*! The windows rattled and the house shook as if it was going to come down and old Brer Bear he fell out of the rocking-chair—*kerblump*!

When the creatures got sort of settled, Brer Possum and Brer Mink, they up and allow that Brer Rabbit got such a monstrous bad cold,

they believe they'll step out and get some fresh air, but the other creatures, they say they going to stick it out; and after a while, they begin to chat among themselves again.

About that time Brer Rabbit, he sing out, 'When a big man like me wants to sneeze, whereabouts he going to sneeze?'

Then the other creatures, they holler back, as if they're cross, 'Big man or little man, sneeze where you please.'

Then Brer Rabbit, he squeal out, 'This is the way a big man sneeze!' and with that he tilted over the tub of dirty water, and when the other creatures hear it come a-sloshing down the stair-steps, gentlemens! they just hoisted themselves out of there. Some of them went out the front door, and some of them fell out of the windows; some went one way and some went another way; but they all went sailing out.

Brer Rabbit he just took and shut up the house and fastened the windows, and then he go to bed, he did, and pull the coverlet up round his ears, and he slept like a man that owes nobody nothing. And neither does he owe them, 'cause if them other creatures are going to get scared and run off from their own house, what business is that of Brer Rabbit?" said Uncle Remus.

Brer Fox
SHINGLES HIS ROOF

"I T appears," said Uncle Remus, "that Brer Rabbit went and put a steeple on top of his house; so all the other creatures want to fix up their houses. Some put new cellars under them, some slapped on new window-blinds, some one thing and some another, but old Brer Fox he took a notion that he'd put some new shingles on the roof.

Brer Rabbit he hear tell of this, and nothing'd do but he must rack round and see how old Brer Fox is getting on. When he got to Brer Fox's house, he hear a mighty lamming and a-bamming and lo and behold, there was Brer Fox sitting straddled on the gable of the roof nailing on shingles just as hard as he can.

Brer Rabbit cast his eye around and he see Brer Fox's dinner sitting in the corner of the fence. It was covered up in a brand new tin pail and it look so nice, that Brer Rabbit's mouth began to water and he allow to himself that he'd like to eat that dinner.

Then Brer Rabbit hail Brer Fox and ask him how he come on. Brer Fox allow he's too busy to hold any confab. Brer Rabbit up and ask him what he's doing up there. Brer Fox allow that he's putting the roof on the house before the rainy season sets in. Brer Rabbit, he up and ask Brer Fox if he ain't in need of some help. Brer Fox he allow that if he is in

need of any help, he don't know where in the name of goodness he's
going to get it.

With that, Brer Rabbit sort of pull his whiskers and say that he used
to be a mighty handy man with a hammer, and he ain't too proud to
whirl in and help Brer Fox.

Brer Fox, he allow he'd be much obliged and no sooner does he say
that than Brer Rabbit snatched off his coat and leapt up the ladder, and
sat in there and put on more shingles in one hour than Brer Fox can put
on in two.

He nailed on shingles till he got tired, Brer Rabbit did, and all the time
he's nailing, he study how he's going to get that dinner. He nailed and he
nailed. He'd nail one row and Brer Fox'd nail another row. He nailed
and he nailed. He catched Brer Fox and passed him—catched him and
passed him, till while he's nailing along, Brer Fox's tail gets in the way.

Brer Rabbit allow to himself that he don't know what in the name of
goodness folks have such long tails for, and he push it out of the way.
He no sooner push it out of the way before here it come back in the way.

They nailed and they nailed, and, bless your soul! 'twasn't long before
Brer Fox drop everything and squall out, 'Laws a massy, Brer Rabbit!
You done nail my tail! Help me, Brer Rabbit! You done nail my tail!'

Brer Rabbit, he say, 'Surely I ain't nail your tail, Brer Fox! Surely not! Look right close, Brer Fox!'

Brer Fox, he holler, he squall, he kick, he squeal. 'Laws a massy, Brer Rabbit! You done nailed my tail! Unnail me, Brer Rabbit, unnail me!'

Brer Rabbit, he make for the ladder, and when he start down, he look at Brer Fox like he's right down sorry and he say, 'Well, well, well! Just to think that I should have lammed a-loose and nailed Brer Fox's tail! I dunno when I hear tell of anything that makes me feel so mighty bad!'

Brer Fox holler, Brer Fox howl, yet it don't do no good. There he was with his tail nailed hard and fast.

Brer Rabbit, he keep on talking whiles he's going down the ladder. 'It makes me feel so mighty bad,' says he, 'that I dunno what to do. Every time I think on it, it makes an empty place come in my stomach,' says Brer Rabbit, says he.

By this time Brer Rabbit is down on the ground and whiles Brer Fox is hollering, he just keeps on a-talking. 'There's a mighty empty place in my stomach,' says he, 'and if I ain't made any mistakes there's a tin-pail full of food in the corner of this here fence that'll just about fit it,' says old Brer Rabbit, says he.

He open the pail and he eat the greens and sup up the molasses and when he wipe his mouth on his coat-tail, he up and allow, 'I dunno when I been so sorry about anything, as I is about Brer Fox's nice long tail. Surely, surely my head must have been wool-gathering when I took and nailed Brer Fox's fine long tail,' says old Brer Rabbit, says he.

And with that, he took and skipped out.''

HOW BRER RABBIT LOST HIS FINE BUSHY TAIL

"ONE time," said Uncle Remus, "old man Rabbit was going along down the road shaking his long bushy tail, and feeling mighty biggity."

"Great goodness, Uncle Remus!" exclaimed the little boy, "everybody knows that rabbits haven't got long bushy tails!"

"Well," said Uncle Remus, "all I know is that this day, old Brer Rabbit was going down the big road shaking his long bushy tail, when who should he strike up with but old Brer Fox ambling along with a big string of fish. Brer Rabbit he open up the confab, he did, and he ask Brer Fox where he got that nice string of fish, and Brer Fox he up and respond that he catched them, and Brer Rabbit say whereabouts, and Brer Fox he say down at the creek, and Brer Rabbit he ask how, and Brer Fox he up and tell Brer Rabbit that all he had to do to get a big pile of fish was to go to the creek after sun-down and drop his tail in the water and sit there till daylight, and then draw up a whole armful of fishes.

So Brer Rabbit set out that night and went a-fishing. The weather was sort of cold, and when he got there he pick out a good place, and he sort of squat down, he did, and let his tail hang in the water. He sat there and he sat there and he think he's going to freeze, but by and by day came

and there he was. He make a pull and he feels as if he's coming in two. He fetch another jerk and lo and behold, where was his tail?"

There was a long pause.

"Did it come off, Uncle Remus?" asked the little boy presently.

"It did that!" replied the old man. "It did that, it froze solid and broke

off! And that's where all the bob-tail rabbits that you see hopping and skedaddling through the woods came from."

"Are they all that way just because the old Rabbit lost his tail in the creek?" asked the little boy.

"That's it, honey," replied the old man. "It looks like they all take after their pa!"

The BAG in the CORNER

"ONE time," said Uncle Remus, "Brer Fox was going down the big road, and he look ahead and he see old Brer Terrapin making his way home. Brer Fox allow this is a mighty good time to nab old Brer Terrapin, and no sooner does he think it than he put out for home, which wasn't far away, and he gets him a bag. He come back, he did, and he run up behind old Brer Terrapin and flip him in the bag and sling the bag across his back and go galloping towards home.

Brer Terrapin, he holler, but that do no good, he rip and he roar, but that do no good. And Brer Fox just keep on a-going.

But whiles all this was going on, Brer Rabbit was sitting right there in the bushes, by the side of the road, and when he see Brer Fox go trotting by, he ask himself what has that creature got in that there bag?

He ask himself, he did, but he dunno the answer. He wonder and he wonder, yet the more he wonder the more he dunno. By and by, he allow to himself, he did, that Brer Fox ain't got no business to be trotting along down the road, toting things which other folk don't know what they is, and he allow that there won't be no great harm done if he go after Brer Fox and find out what he's got in that there bag.

With that, Brer Rabbit he set out. He took a short cut, and before Brer Fox got home, Brer Rabbit had time to go round by the water-melon patch and do some of his mischief. Then he sat down in the bushes where he can see Brer Fox when he come home.

By and by here come Brer Fox with the bag slung across his back. He unlatch the door, he did, and he go and sling Brer Terrapin down in the corner and sat down in front of the fire to rest himself.

Brer Fox had no more than lit his pipe before Brer Rabbit stick his head in the door and holler, 'Brer Fox! Oh, Brer Fox! You better take your walking-stick and run down yonder. There's a whole parcel of folks in your water-melon patch, just a-tramping round and a-tearing down. I hollered at them, but they don't pay no attention to a little man like I is. Make haste, Brer Fox, make haste! Get your stick and run down there. You better make haste, Brer Fox, if you want to get the good of your water-melons. Run, Brer Fox, run!'

With that Brer Rabbit dart back in the bushes and Brer Fox drop his pipe and grab his walking-stick and put out for the water-melon patch; and no sooner is he gone than old Brer Rabbit come out of the bushes and make his way into the house.

He look around and there was the bag in the corner. He catched hold of the bag and sort of feel it, and every time he do this, he hear something holler, 'Ow! Go 'way! Let me alone! Turn me loose! Ow!'

Brer Rabbit jump back astonished. Then before you can wink your eyeball, Brer Rabbit slap himself on the leg and break out in a laugh. Then he allow, 'If I don't make no mistakes, that kind of fuss can come from nobody in the round world but old Brer Terrapin!'

Brer Terrapin, he holler, 'Ain't that Brer Rabbit?'

'The same,' says he.

'Then whirl in and turn me out. There's meal dust in my throat and grit in my eye, and I can't get my breath, scarcely. Turn me out, Brer Rabbit,' says Brer Terrapin, talking like somebody down in a well.

Brer Rabbit begin to laugh, and he keep on laughing, and he laugh till he had his fill of laughing; and then he took and untied the bag and take Brer Terrapin out and tote him away off into the woods. Then, when he done this, Brer Rabbit run off and get a great big hornet's nest that he see when he coming along. Brer Rabbit slap his hand over the little hole in the hornet's nest, then he took it to Brer Fox's house, and put it in the bag where Brer Terrapin had been.

Yet before he put the bag back in the corner," continued Uncle Remus, "what does that creature do? That there creature grab the bag and slam it down against the floor, and hit it against the side of the house till he get them hornets all stirred up, and then he put the bag back in the corner and go out in the bushes where Brer Terrapin is waiting, and then both of them sat out there and wait to see what the upshot's going to be.

By and by, here come Brer Fox back from his water-melon patch, and he look like he's mighty mad. He strike his stick down upon the ground, like he's going to take his revengeance out of poor old Brer Terrapin. He went in the door, Brer Fox did, and shut it after him. Brer Rabbit and Brer Terrapin listen, but they hear nothing.

But by and by, they hear the most audacious racket. It seems like a whole parcel of cows is running round in Brer Fox's house. They hear the chairs a-falling, and the table turning over, and the crockery breaking and then the door flew open and out come Brer Fox a-squalling as if Old Nick was after him. And such a sight as them other creatures see, ain't never been seen before or since.

Them hornets swarmed on top of Brer Fox. Eleven dozen of them would hit him at one time. They bit him and they stung him, and it look like that creature's going to find out for himself what pain and suffering is.

Brer Rabbit and Brer Terrapin, they sat there, and they laugh and laugh, till by and by Brer Rabbit roll over and grab his stomach and holler, 'Don't, Brer Terrapin, don't! One giggle more and you'll have to tote me!' ''

Brer Coon and the frogs

"ONE time," said Uncle Remus, "Brer Rabbit and Brer Coon lived in the same neighbourhood. Brer Rabbit, he was a fisherman, and Brer Coon, he was a fisherman, but Brer Rabbit, he catched fish, and Brer Coon, he fished for frogs. Brer Rabbit, he had mighty good luck, and Brer Coon, he had mighty bad luck. Brer Rabbit, he got fat and sleek, and Brer Coon, he got poor and sick.

It went on this-a-way till one day Brer Coon meet Brer Rabbit in the big road. They shook hands, they did, and then Brer Coon, he allow, 'Brer Rabbit, where you get such a fine catch of fish?' Brer Rabbit laugh and say, 'I catched them out of the river, Brer Coon. All I've got to do is bait my hook,' says he.

Then Brer Coon shake his head and allow. 'Then how come I can't catch no frogs? How in the name of goodness can I catch them, Brer Rabbit? I'd like to have something to eat for me and my family con-nection.'

Brer Rabbit sort of grin and then he say, 'Well, Brer Coon, seeing as you been so friendly with me and never showed your toothies when I pull your tail, I'll just whirl in and help you out.'

Brer Coon say, 'Thanky, thanky-do, Brer Rabbit.'

Brer Rabbit hung his fish on the branch of a tree and say, 'Now Brer Coon, you must do just like I tell you.'

Brer Coon allowed that he would, if he was spared.

Then Brer Rabbit say, 'Now, Brer Coon, you just rack down yonder and get on the big sand-bank, twixt the river and the stream. When you get there you must stagger like you're sick, and then you must whirl round and round and drop down like you're dead. After you drop down, you must sort of jerk your legs once or twice, and then you must lie right still. If a fly light on your nose, let him stay there. Don't move; don't wink your eye; don't switch your tail. Just lie right there, and 'twon't be long before you hear from me. Yet don't you move till I give the word.'

Brer Coon, he paced off, he did, and done just as Brer Rabbit told him. He staggered round on the sand-bank and then he dropped down dead. After a time Brer Rabbit come loping along, and as soon as he got there, he squall out, 'Coon's dead!'

This roused the frogs and they stuck their heads up to see what all the noise was about. One big green one up and holler, 'What's the matter? What's the matter?' He talked like he had a bad cold.

Brer Rabbit allow, 'Coon's dead!'

Frog say, 'Don't believe it! Don't believe it!'

Another frog say, 'Yes, he is! Yes, he is!'

Little bit of a one say, 'No, he ain't! No, he ain't!'

They keep on disputing and disputing till by and by it seems like all the frogs in the neighbourhood were there. Brer Rabbit look like he ain't a-hearing or a-caring what they do or say. He sat there in the sand like he was a-mourning for Brer Coon. The frogs kept getting closer and closer. Brer Coon, he don't move. When a fly get on him, Brer Rabbit, he'd brush it off.

By and by he allow, 'If you want to get him out of the way, now's your time, Cousin Frogs. Just whirl in and bury him deep in the sand.'

Big old frog say, 'How we going to do it? How we going to do it?'

Brer Rabbit allow, 'Dig the sand out from under him and let him down in the hole.'

Then the frogs they went to work sure enough. There must have been a hundred of 'em, and they make that sand fly, man! Brer Coon, he don't move. The frogs, they dig and scratch in the sand till after a while they had a right smart hole, and Brer Coon was down in there.

By and by, big frog holler, 'This deep enough? This deep enough?'

Brer Rabbit ask, 'Can you jump out?'

Big frog say, 'Yes, I can! Yes, I can!'

Brer Rabbit say, 'Then 'tain't deep enough.'

Then the frogs they dig and they dig till by and by big frog say, 'This deep enough? This deep enough?'

Brer Rabbit ask, 'Can you jump out?'

Big frog say, 'I just can! I just can!'

Brer Rabbit say, 'Dig it deeper!'

The frogs keep on digging until by and by big frog holler out, 'This deep enough? This deep enough?'

Brer Rabbit ask, 'Can you jump out?'

Big frog say, 'No, I can't! I can't! Come help me! Come help me!'

Brer Rabbit burst out laughing and holler out, 'Rise up, Brer Coon and get your supper!'

And Brer Coon rise."

TROUBLE
in the
FOX FAMILY

"ONE day," said Uncle Remus, "Brer Rabbit come to the cross-roads when who should he meet but old Brer Fox, and not only Brer Fox but two fat pullets. Brer Rabbit, he said howdy and Brer Fox he said hello and they jawed awhile, and about the time that Brer Fox was going to say so-long, Brer Rabbit, after feeling in his pockets and looking like he done lost something, pull out a piece of paper and hold it up. He allow, 'I was to show you this when I see you.'

Brer Fox he look at it kind of sideways. He say, 'Is there any writing on it? 'Cause if there is, it ain't going to do me no good to look at it: I can read reading, but I can't read writing.'

Brer Rabbit say that's the case with him, 'cepting that he can read writing, but he can't read reading.

Brer Fox, he ask, he did, 'What does the writing say?'

Brer Rabbit, he kind of wrinkle up his forehead and hold out the paper like you've seen old folks do. He pretend he's reading, and he allow, ''Tain't nothing at all but a summons to come to the court-house.'

Brer Fox ask if he got time to take his meat home, and Brer Rabbit allow that he has. With that Brer Fox made off down the road and Brer

46

Rabbit followed along after Brer Fox, but he took care to keep out of sight.

He see'd Brer Fox run into his house to put the pullets away, then he run out again. Brer Rabbit stayed where he was until Brer Fox was gone, and then he sauntered out in the big road and made his way to Brer Fox's house. He went up, he did, monstrous polite—it look like butter won't melt in his mouth. He went to the door and rap on it and stand there with his hat in his hand, and look mighty humble-come-tumble.

Old Missis Fox, she open the door, and Brer Rabbit say he got a message for her somewheres in his pocket, if he can find it. After a long time he find the paper. He hand her this, and Missis Fox say she ain't a good hand at reading, not since the chillun broke her far-seeing specs.

Then Brer Rabbit up and tell her that he met Brer Fox, and Brer Fox ask him how he was getting on and Brer Rabbit say he'd be getting on pretty well if he had anything to eat at his house. Then Brer Fox wipe his eye and say it won't do for Brer Rabbit to go without eating.

Old Missis Fox break into the tale with, 'I wish he'd wipe his eye about some of my troubles, his eye is dry enough when he's round here.'

Brer Rabbit allow, 'Yes'm,' and then he say that Brer Fox allow as how that very morning he fetched home two fat pullets, and he say Brer Rabbit can have them. More than that Brer Rabbit say Brer Fox sat right flat in the road and wrote Missis Fox a note so that she'll know his will and desirements.

Old Missis Fox say that if the letter ain't read till she reads it, she mighty sorry for the letter. She took it and turn it upper-side down and round and round and then hand it back to Brer Rabbit. 'What does it say?' says she.

Brer Rabbit he cleared his throat and make out he's reading. 'To all whom it might contrive and concern both now and presently, be so pleased as to let Brer Rabbit have the pullets. I'm well at this writing and hoping you're enjoying the same shower of blessings.'

Missis Fox ain't pleased with the letter, but she fetch the two fat pullets, and Brer Rabbit, he made for home.

Brer Fox he can't find anybody at the court-house, and after so long he come back home. Missis Fox began to jaw him long before he got in listening distance. Brer Fox don't say nothing. Soon as she can catch her breath, she allow. 'What make you fetch home food if you going to send it off again? What business you got sending the two fine fat pullets to old Missis Rabbit? I ain't no more than seen them, before here come old Brer Rabbit a-bowing and a-scraping and a-simpering and a-sniggering, and he allow that you done sent him for the pullets. If it had just been his own lone say-so, he'd never have got them pullets in the round world, but here he come with a letter what you wrote! How come you giving pullets to Brer Rabbit and his family when your own chillun is going round so thin that they can't make a shadow in the moonshine?'

Brer Fox allow, 'Does you mean to stand there and tell me that you took and give Brer Rabbit them fine fat pullets what I bring home? Does you mean to tell me that?'

She say, 'If I done it, I done it 'cause you write and tell me to do it.'

Brer Fox allow, 'Is you got the impudence to tell me that just 'cause Brer Rabbit hands you a piece of paper with something or other marked on it you ain't got nothing better to do than give him the fine fat pullets what I bring home to make some chicken pie?'

This make old Missis Fox so mad that she can't see straight, and when she can talk plain, she vow she going to hurt Brer Rabbit if it took a lifetime to do it. And there was Brer Fox just as mad, if not madder. They both sat down and ground their toothies and mumble and growl, and by and by Brer Fox say, 'I'm going to get some rabbit meat to make up for the chicken what you done give away. You keep sweeping here in front of the door and whilst you're sweeping, make out you're talking to me like I'm in the house. Brer Rabbit, he'll be coming along the road soon, and I'll come up on him when he ain't thinking about it.'

So said: so done. Missis Fox she sweep and sweep, and whilst she sweeping, she make out she talking to Brer Fox in the house. Just about that time up come Brer Rabbit with a mighty polite bow. He took off his

hat, he did. 'Good evening, Missis Fox. I hope I see you well, ma'am.'

Missis Fox allow that she ain't as well as she might be, and more than that her old man is lying in the house right now with a mighty bad case of influendways.

Brer Rabbit say he was mighty sorry. Then he sort of smile and he up and ask, he did, 'Missis Fox, how you like that calico frock that Brer Fox done brought you?'

Missis Fox lean her broom against the house and put her hands on her hips and make Brer Rabbit repeat what he done told her. 'Well, well, well,' says old Missis Fox, says she, 'a calico frock and I ain't laid eyes on it!'

'You'll have to excuse me, ma'am,' says Brer Rabbit, says he, 'I'm feared I said something I oughtn't to say. Yet Brer Fox is right there in the house and you can ask him if you don't believe me.'

For one long minute Missis Fox was so mad that she had to wait till she catched her breath before she can say a word. Quick as she can she holler out, 'No, he ain't in the house; he's out yonder trying to slip up on you about them pullets!'

With that Brer Rabbit make his bow and light out from there, and he wasn't none too soon either, 'cause he ain't more than got in the bushes where he can hide himself before here comes Brer Fox.

He look all around, but he ain't see nobody but his old woman. Brer Fox say, 'Where is the trifling scoundrel? I see'd him standing right here—where is he?'

Old Missis Fox she up with the broom and sent him a biff on the side of the head that came mighty near knocking him into the next county. 'That's where he is,' says she, and she fetch her old man a whack across the backbone.

Old Brer Fox took a notion that he'd been struck by lightning. He fell down and rolled over, and old Missis Fox had mighty nearly worn the broom out before he find out what was happening. He holler out, 'Why, laws a massy, honey, what's the matter with you? What you biffing me for? *I* ain't Brer Rabbit! Ow! Please, honey, don't bang me so hard!'

Old Missis Fox, says she, 'Where's my fine calico frock?' And all the time she was talking she was wiping him up with the broom.

Well, when Brer Fox got out of reach and she kind of cooled down, she up and ask him about the calico frock, and he vow he ain't seen no calico frock. There they was—no frock and no pullets, and Brer Rabbit still cutting up his capers and playing his pranks on everything and everybody!"

THE MOON
in the
Mill-Pond

"THERE were times," said the old man with a sigh, "when the creatures would all be friendly together. Them was the times when old Brer Rabbit would pretend that he was going to quit his knavishness, and they'd all go round just as though they belonged to the same family connection.

One time, after they had all been agreeing together this-a-way, Brer Rabbit began to feel fidgety. One night after supper he ran into old Brer Terrapin, and after they shook hands they sat down on the side of the road and run on about old times. They talk and they talk, they did, and by and by Brer Rabbit say the time had come when he'd like to have some fun, and Brer Terrapin allow that Brer Rabbit was just the very man he'd been looking for.

'Well, then,' says Brer Rabbit, says he, 'we'll just give Brer Fox and Brer Wolf and Brer Bear special notice, and tomorrow night we'll meet down by the mill-pond and have a little fishing frolic.'

Brer Terrapin laugh. 'If I ain't there,' says he, 'then you may know the grasshopper done fly away with me,' says he.

Next day, Brer Rabbit sent word to all the other creatures, and sure enough, when the time come, they was all there. Brer Bear, he brought a hook and line; Brer Wolf, he brought a hook and line; Brer Fox, he brought a dip-net, and Brer Terrapin, not to be outdone, he fetch the bait.

They get ready, they did, and Brer Rabbit march up to the pond and make to throw his line in the water, but just then, it seem like he sees something. The other creatures, they stop and watch his motions. Brer Rabbit, he drop the rod, he did, and he stand there scratching his head and looking down in the water.

The other creatures begin to get uneasy when they see this and Brer Fox, he up and holler out, 'Law, Brer Rabbit, what in the name of goodness is the matter in there?'

Brer Rabbit scratch his head and look in the water; he keep on scratching and looking.

By and by he took a long breath, he did, and he allow, 'Gentlemens all, we might as well make tracks from this here place, 'cause there ain't no fishing in that pond for none of this here crowd.'

With that Brer Terrapin, he scrambled up to the water's edge and look over, and he shook his head and say, 'To be sure! To be sure! Tut-tut-tut!' and then he crawl back he did.

'Don't be scared,' says Brer Rabbit, 'there ain't nothing much the matter, excepting that the Moon done drop in the water. If you don't believe me you can look for yourselves,' says he.

With that they all went to the bank and looked in; and sure enough there lay the Moon, a-swinging and a-swaying at the bottom of the pond.

Brer Fox, he look in and he allow, 'Well, well, well!'

Brer Wolf he look in and he allow, 'Mighty bad, mighty bad!'

Brer Bear he look in and he allow, 'Tum, tum, tum!'

Brer Rabbit he look in again and he up and allow, he did, 'Gentlemens, you all can hum and haw, but unless we gets that Moon out of the pond there ain't no fish to be catched round here this night; and if you'll ask Brer Terrapin, he'll tell you the same.'

Then they ask how they can get the Moon out of there, and Brer Terrapin allow they better leave that to Brer Rabbit.

Brer Rabbit, he shut his eyes, he did, and seem to be thinking. By and by he up and allow, 'The nearest way out of this here difficulty is to send round to old Mr. Mud Turtle and borrow his big net and drag the Moon up from there,' says he.

'I declare to gracious I mighty glad you mention that,' says Brer Terrapin, says he. 'Mr. Mud Turtle is such a close relation of mine that I calls him Unc' Muck, and I lay if you send there after that net you won't find Unc' Muck so mighty disobliging.'

Well, they sent for the net, and whiles Brer Rabbit was gone, Brer Terrapin he say that time and again he hear tell that them what find the Moon in the water and fetch it out, likewise fetch out a pot of money. This make Brer Fox and Brer Wolf and Brer Bear feel mighty good, and they reckon that seeing Brer Rabbit has been so good as to run after the net, they'll do the netting.

By the time Brer Rabbit got back, he see how the land lay, and he pretend he want to go in after the Moon. He pull off his coat and he was fixing to take off his waistcoat, but the other creatures, they allow they won't let a dry-foot man like Brer Rabbit go in the water. So Brer Fox

he took hold of one end of the net, Brer Wolf he took hold of the other end, and Brer Bear he wade along behind to lift the net over logs and snags.

They made one haul—no Moon; another haul—no Moon; another haul—no Moon. Then by and by they go out further from the bank. Water run in Brer Fox's ear, he shake his head; water run in Brer Wolf's ear, he shake his head; water run in Brer Bear's ear, he shake his head. And the first news you know, whiles they was a-shaking, they come to where the bottom shelved steeply. Brer Fox he step off and duck himself; then Brer Wolf duck himself, and Brer Bear, he make a splunge and duck himself, and bless gracious, they kick and splatter till it look like they was going to slosh all the water out of the mill-pond.

When they came out, there weren't no worse-looking creatures than them. Brer Rabbit holler, 'I 'spect you all, gents, better go home and get some dry duds, and another time we'll be in better luck,' says he. 'I hear tell that the Moon will bite at a hook if you use fools for bait, and I lay that's the only way to catch her,' says he.

Brer Fox and Brer Wolf and Brer Bear went dripping off, and Brer Rabbit and Brer Terrapin and the others, they went home laughing.''

Little
MR.
CRICKET

"M R. CRICKET ain't so mighty big," said Uncle Remus, "but he's big enough to make a heap of fuss in the world. This Mr. Cricket never had a chance to live in a chimney-corner. He stayed out in the bushes and the high grass, and he didn't do nothing in the round world but play on his fife and his fiddle. When he got tired of one, he'd turn to the other.

Little Mr. Cricket went on this-a-way till the cool nights and days began to come on, and sometimes he had to warm himself by getting under a clump of grass. But he was very cheerful; he ain't dropped no sobs and he ain't shed no sighs and he kept on a-fluting and a-fiddling.

One day when the sun was shining kind of thankful-like, he climbed on top of the tall grass and fiddled away like somebody was frying meat. He hear someone coming, and he look right close, and lo and behold! it was old Brer Fox.

He allow, 'Hello, Brer Fox! Where you going?'

Brer Fox kind of pull himself up and ask, 'Who's that?'

Little Mr. Cricket say, 'It ain't nobody in the round world but me. I know I ain't much, but I'm mighty lively when the sun shines hot. Where you going, Brer Fox?'

Brer Fox he say, 'I'm going where I'm going, that's where I'm going, and I wouldn't be too much astonished if I was to land in town for to get my dinner. I used to be a rover in my young days, and I'm still a-roving.'

'Well, well,' says little Mr. Cricket, says he, 'I used to belong to the rover family myself, but now I done settle down and don't do a thing in the world but have my fun in my own way. But since I see you and hear you talk so gaily, I done took a notion to take dinner in town myself.'

Brer Fox allow, 'How will you get there, little friend?'

Mr. Cricket say, 'Ain't you never watched my motions? I got legs and feet and I catched the jumping habit from old Cousin Grasshopper. What time you 'spect to get to town?'

Brer Fox respond, 'Give me two good hours, and I'll be right there with my appetite with me.'

Little Mr. Cricket seem like he was astonished. He held up all his hands and mighty nearly all his feet. 'Two hours! Well, by the time you get there, I'll have had my dinner and be ready to take my nap.'

Brer Fox grin at him and allow, 'If you'll beat me so much as ten inches, I'll pay for your dinner and let you choose your own food. If I beat you, why then you'll have to provide the dinner.'

Little Mr. Cricket say he'll be more than glad to carry out that programme. And then Brer Fox after grinning again loped off. But just before Brer Fox made his start, little Mr. Cricket made his: he took a flying jump and landed on Brer Fox's big, bushy tail, and there he stayed.

When Brer Fox had been going a little more than an hour, he meet Brer Rabbit on the road, and they said howdy. Brer Fox laugh and up and tell Brer Rabbit about the race betwixt him and Mr. Cricket.

Old Brer Rabbit, he rolled his eyeballs and looked so funny that Brer Fox ask him what is the matter with him.

'I was just wondering,' says Brer Rabbit, says he, 'how you'd feel to find Mr. Cricket there before you. The smart little creature passed me on the road a quarter of an hour ago. If you're going to get there ahead of him, you'll have to whip up your horses. What you been doing all this time? You must have fallen asleep and didn't know it.'

Brer Fox panted. 'No, sir, I been coming full tilt all the time.'

Brer Rabbit respond, 'Then all I got to say is that Mr. Cricket has got

a mighty knack for getting over the ground. I 'spect he done got there by this time.'

'If he ain't,' says Brer Fox, says he, 'I'll catch him,' and with that he went off just as hard as he can. But fast as he went, Mr. Cricket was going just as fast. I dunno but what he had gone fast asleep in the soft bed where he was hiding.

When Brer Rabbit see Brer Fox mend his pace, he just roll over and wallow in the sand and laugh fit to kill himself. He say to himself, 'I'm mighty glad I met my old friend 'cause now I know that all the fools ain't dead—and long may they live to give me something to do. I don't know how in the wide world I'd get along without them. They keeps me fat and saucy whether times are good or not!' 'Cause when Brer Rabbit was looking Brer Fox over, his eye fell on little Mr. Cricket, and that's what made him laugh.

Well, the upshot of the whole business was that when Brer Fox got to town, Mr. Cricket took a flying jump and holler out, 'Heyo, Brer Fox! Where you been all this time? You must have stopped somewhere on the road to get your dinner. And I'm sorry too, I had mine so long ago that I'm about ready and willing to eat again. I had the idea from what you said that you was going to come on as hard as you could. You must have stopped on the way and had a confab with Brer Rabbit. I met him on the way, and it look to me that he was ready to pass the time of day with anybody that came along.'

Brer Fox was astonished. He say, 'How in the world did you get here so quick, Mr. Cricket?'

Mr. Cricket, he make answer, 'I can hardly tell you, Brer Fox. You know how I travels—with a hop, skip and jump—well, I hopped, skipped and jumped a little quicker this time and got here all safe and sound. When old acquaintance holler at me on the road, I just kept on a-going. I found out long ago that the way to get anywhere is to go on where you're going.'

Brer Fox shook his head, and panted, and he run his hand in his pocket and paid for Mr. Cricket's dinner: and then after dinner Mr. Cricket sat back and took a chew of tobacco and warmed himself in the sun."

© *First Edition 1969*
ISBN 0 00 138188 1
PRINTED AND MADE IN GREAT BRITAIN BY
WM. COLLINS SONS AND CO. LTD. LONDON, GLASGOW

Brer Bear

Brer Coo[n]

Brer Squirrel

Mrs. Brer Fox

Brer Rabbit

Mr. Dog